Roses & Thorns

(A Rose Trilogy Short-Story)

I0538287

by

Tish Thawer

Amber Leaf Publishing
Missouri, USA

Roses & Thorns Copyright© 2012 by Tish Thawer. All rights reserved. No part of this book may be used or reproduced in any manner whatsoever, including Internet usage, without written permission from Amber Leaf Publishing, except in the case of brief quotations embodied in articles and reviews.

First Edition
First Printing, 2012
ISBN: 978-0-9856703-1-3

Library of Congress Control Number: 2012909479

Front cover designed by Regina Wamba of Mae I Design and Photography
Full-wrap design by Emma Michaels
Free stock photo of woman courtesy of Marcus Ranum / ranum.com
Edited by Kara Malinczak

This is a work of fiction. Names, characters, places, organizations, and events portrayed in this novel are either products of the author's imagination or are used fictitiously. And any resemblance to actual persons (living or dead), business establishments, or locales is entirely coincidental. Any brand names have been used under the Fair Use Act.

Amber Leaf Publishing, Missouri, USA
www.amberleafpublishing.com
www.tishthawer.com

Roses & Thorns

(A Rose Trilogy Short-Story)

A flash back to how Rose and Christian's whirlwind romance started, as they build the relationship that will see them through the difficult times that lie ahead.

Acknowledgements

Thanks again to my entire family. I would be lost without you.

To all my friends at Shelfari, your support has been amazing!

To Regina Wamba, Emma Michaels, and Kara Malinczak—You are my angels.

And to Cortney—I've finally found my lost twin.

CHAPTER ONE

Best Concert Ever

(Rose)

"Oh my god, that was the best concert EVER!" Penny yelled.

"I know, right? I've never screamed and danced so much in my life," said Jillian.

My friends and I had just left the Nine Inch Nails concert in Masen and were being driven home in one of my dad's company limos. It was Friday night and since we'd be off from school Monday as well, this was the perfect start to a long weekend. We didn't have a curfew, but since some of us still weren't twenty-one, and since there really wasn't anything fun to do at two in the morning, we were headed back to Jillian's where we'd all be spending the night.

Suddenly, Jillian announced, "I've got to pee."

As the girls continued to giggle and drink more of the complementary soda–*Dad had made sure that all alcohol had been removed*–I pushed the button for the intercom. "Excuse me. Is there somewhere we could stop to use the restroom? Apparently, it's an emergency."

After a moment's pause, our driver's voice came through the speaker. "Yes ma'am. There's a nightclub just up the road. It's the only place close by, so I'll stop there if that's okay?"

"Yes. Thank you. That will be fine." Jillian was the only one in our group that was already twenty-one, so stopping at a nightclub wouldn't be a problem.

We drove for a few more miles and then coasted to a stop. As I looked out the tinted window, I saw the club's sign lit up in bright red lights. *The Rising Pit*.

One of the "car crew" got out and opened the side

door. Jill hurriedly climbed out of the car and gave a little wave to the driver. "Thank you." She then followed her escort towards the front door.

"I can't believe your dad set all this up, Rose. It's really cool. I haven't had this much fun in a long time. Thanks for inviting me," Penny said.

"You're welcome. I was really surprised when he told me that we'd be going in one of the company limos. I hadn't realized at the time that it would come with a babysitting crew though," I joked.

I knew that my dad had made sure that our escorts would be keeping us in their sights all night, and I thought that it would be a pain in the ass, but really it hadn't bothered me at all. They were all very nice, and there was one that was pretty damn cute, too. The one that had just accompanied Jillian inside, actually.

I looked back to the club just as Jill and the cutie

disappeared behind the door. I watched as a man stepped outside carrying a girl in his arms. He placed her on her feet, steadying her before letting go. It looked like she was crying. As he talked to her, she wiped the tears from her cheeks and then gave a quick nod of her head and smiled. Obviously, whatever the man had said was making her feel better. It was obvious the guy worked there since he had a black t-shirt on with the club's name and logo on the front. I continued to watch, wondering what could have happened that would leave a club employee comforting a crying patron on the front steps, but the moment the man smiled, my curiosity was forgotten.

It was as if the heavens were highlighting my destiny for me. The clouds broke, and suddenly it wasn't just a "man" I was staring at...it was an angel. He was so gorgeous. He had to be about 6' 2", and solid muscle from the looks of him. Not bulky like those beefed-up body builders, but very athletic. Wide shoulders, broad chest, thin waist, and what I was sure would be strong, muscled legs. With the moonlight shining on him, I could see he had dark blonde hair with golden highlights, cut short and sharp. I realized I was half-hanging out the open window of the limo. I sucked in a quick breath, and that's when he suddenly turned and looked right at me. I thought I would die.

His eyes were so beautiful and so mesmerizing. They were an amber color, a rich brown with golden highlights, mixing together like swirled caramel and honey. The intensity of his gaze was piercing. He was easily the most beautiful thing I'd ever seen.

Jill came barreling out of the nightclub with her escort closely in tow. We all started busting up laughing as we heard her say, "I only wanted a quick shot." I continued to stare at the gorgeous man as she started to make her way back to the limo, but as she walked past him, he reached out and tapped her gently on the shoulder. I continued to watch, jealousy filling my veins, as she stopped and started to speak to him. I couldn't imagine what they could possibly be talking about, but she kept glancing at the car and then back to him with a huge smile on her face. I'm sure she was trying to make sure we were all seeing that this beautiful man was paying attention to her. I loved Jill, but she could definitely be an attention whore sometimes. After a brief moment, I saw him hand her something and then he walked back inside. My angel was gone.

I settled myself back in the limo, trying not to let the stickiness of the leather seats on my bare legs elevate my frustration as I anxiously waited for my best friend to come brag about how this impossibly gorgeous guy had just asked her out or something. I tried to convince myself that their conversation had only been about her using the facilities instead of being a paying customer, but I doubted that was really the case.

When Jill got in the car, she sat there for a moment with a cat-ate-the-mouse grin on her face that I wanted to smack off, but then she handed me a business card. I was confused and almost handed it back without looking at it, but she just sat there smiling, so I quickly looked down and examined the shiny card. It had the club's logo on the front, which looked like a square hatch opening up with a bright red glow shining from within, and the club's name, *The Rising Pit*, printed above it. The moment I turned it over however, is the moment my life changed. The first thing I noticed was a handwritten note that started with my name. Now I was interested. It said, "Roses are red, but I'll be blue, if I'm denied the pleasure, of meeting you. ~ Christian."

I read it about three times before I looked up and saw that Jillian was still smiling at me. She grabbed the card out of my hand and passed it to my friends. "He asked me your name and then scratched out that poem so fast that I could barely see his hand move. His number's on there too and he said for you to call him after dark in two days."

I was stunned into silence. I couldn't understand how this extraordinary man could possibly want to meet me. *Me!* Not that I wasn't thrilled, but suddenly I was so nervous that I didn't think I could survive two days without losing my mind. My thoughts drifted to the first thing a girl thinks of when preparing to meet her dream guy...what was I going to wear?

My friend's laughter and Jillian's question brought my attention back to the present. "Holy crap, Rose. Are you gonna call him?"

I thought for a moment then answered, "Hell yes, I'm gonna call him! He's frickin' gorgeous."

The girl's conversations quickly became background noise as I stared out the window. *Why would this incredible man want to meet me?* I couldn't help but wonder if calling a complete stranger was a monumental mistake. But, as the butterflies increased their pace in my stomach, I glanced out the window again and could have sworn that I saw Christian's golden swirled eyes staring back at me from the reflection. *Hell yes I was going to call him.* And suddenly...two days seemed like an eternity.

CHAPTER TWO

Shopping

(Rose)

I pulled the covers over my head and squinted my eyes against the sunlight that was now blaring in from behind the curtains my mother had just yanked open.

"Rise and shine. We're going shopping." Mom's enthusiasm exhausted me. She was so upbeat all the time, and while I loved that about her, it was something that got old really fast. Especially when you'd planned to use Sunday to recuperate from a sleepless night spent with your friends after a rowdy concert. "Come on, Rose. I want to hit the sales at Kohl's before all the good stuff is gone. They've slashed prices on all their swim wear, and I'm in serious need of some new suits."

I watched her dark hair sway just below her shoulders as she bounced towards my closet.

"Alright, alright. But can you give me a few minutes to actually wake up first?" Mom's cocked hip and the angle of her head as she spun around and threw a dress onto my bed was an indication that her answer was no. I narrowed my eyes at her as I jumped out of bed, grabbed the dress, and stomped into the bathroom.

Fumbling through a rushed version of my morning routine, I quickly combed through my long blonde hair and stuck a hat on my head. A little mineral powder on my cheeks and some tinted lip gloss was going to be the extent of my makeup efforts this morning. I emerged dressed and ready to go in just a few minutes.

As I made my way downstairs, I heard a commotion in the kitchen and headed in the direction of the noise. I suddenly wished I had taken longer to get ready. Mom and Dad were saying their goodbyes for the morning, but from the way his hands were grabbing at her and the intensity of their kiss, you'd think we were leaving for a yearlong safari in Africa, instead of an afternoon of shopping a few miles away.

I cleared my throat as I slipped on my flip-flops. "Okay, I'm ready."

Mom broke off their passionate kiss and backed out of Dad's embrace with a huge smile on her face. "Okay, let's hit it." She gave Dad a little wave as she headed out the door. It must have been her who initiated their dramatic goodbye scene, because Dad stood there frozen in place and then he started laughing.

I shook my head and grabbed my purse from the hook next to the wooden credenza by the door. "Bye Dad, catch ya later!" I said as I rushed to follow Mom to the car.

"Bye, honey. Try to keep your mother's spending in check for me, will ya?" he hollered out the door.

I knew he was kidding because he never did anything to "keep mother in check." My parents loved each other so much, and they both had successful careers, so money wasn't really a big deal. It's not like we were super-rich, but we didn't have to worry about overspending on a sale at Kohl's, that was for sure.

"So, what else are we doing today besides shopping for swimsuits?" I asked.

"Well, I thought we could get some lunch and you could tell me all about your concert. I talked to Adrienne this morning and she said you guys were all pretty excited when you arrived at her house."

"Yes, we had a really good time. The concert was great." I only debated a moment before deciding to tell her about Christian. My mom and I have always had a really close relationship. "But I was actually more excited about the guy I met on the way home."

"Oh, really?" Her coy smile was the first indication that this shopping trip was actually just a recognizance mission. She must have found the business card in my things already.

"Yes. If you don't already know, his name is Christian, and he works at The Rising Pit. As a matter of fact, I'm supposed to call him tonight."

She giggled as we turned the corner and headed towards the end of the shopping district that had the best little breakfast café in it. "Yes, I found the business card in your things when I was cleaning up this morning, and that's why I thought we could buy you something nice to wear today." She glanced in my direction, probably to see if I was mad that she had "cleaned" my things, but I wasn't. Like I said, there wasn't much that I hid from my parents.

"That sounds great. Didn't you just love his little poem?" I asked.

"Yes, it reminded me of when your dad and I first met and the little romantic thing that he did to win my attention."

"Aha...is that why you practically attacked him before we left this morning? Were you reminiscing?" I laughed as I watched Mom shake her head. Obviously, I had pin-pointed the reason for her behavior.

"Yes!" she declared with a hint of shyness in her voice.

"Well, I think it's cute. I can only hope that when I meet "the one," that we will be as in love as you and Dad are."

At the mention of *love*, Mom's tone turned serious. "I wish that for you too, Rose. Follow your heart, but just be careful. That's the best advice I can give. You're not a child anymore, and the fact that you'll be graduating college this year only adds to the pressure of growing up, but you need to take the time to really live. Enjoy your life. Meeting new boys and having fun is something that I want for you, but I'm also your mom and that means I worry about you at the same time."

"Don't worry, Mom. I'm going to call him after dark like he asked, and then hopefully he'll invite me down to meet him. Will I be able to borrow the car?"

"Yes, that will be fine."

"Okay, thanks. If I do end up going down, I'll feel pretty safe since we'll be in a place where there are a lot of other people around. Plus, I don't know why, but for some reason I just feel like he's going to be a *really* great guy."

"Well, I hope you're right. Now how about some

breakfast? I'm starving."

"Sounds great." As a matter of fact, *everything* was sounding great. Mom was on board with me meeting Christian for the first time, she and Dad were perfectly happy as usual, and I was graduating college early this year. Yes, everything was perfect. Now I just hoped that things would stay that way.

CHAPTER THREE

Get Ready

(Christian)

Long blonde hair, beautiful blue eyes, and a mouth I was dying to kiss were the first things that entered my mind as I awoke for the night.

Being a vampire came with a few neat tricks, and this was one of them. Whatever our last thought was before we fell asleep, was also the first thing we thought of when we woke up. For the last two days I had made it a point to think of Rose.

Two nights ago, I'd carried Sari out of the club, trying to sooth her broken heart. As I sat her on her feet, I was met with the most delectable scent drifting on the wind. Wanting to be a gentleman, I focused on Sari and tried to explain that Bobby wasn't trying to be mean, but that she needed to understand he was a free spirit and she was just going to have to accept that if she wanted to remain a part of his life. But what I had truly wanted to do was search the area and envelop myself in what or whoever was the cause of that delicious smell.

As Sari wiped her tears, I smiled at her and was met with the sound of someone taking a quick breath. *There.* There she was. The most beautiful woman I had ever laid eyes on was practically hanging out the window of a limo. She looked like an angel sent straight from heaven.

Just then, I caught a whiff of the same smell as a couple started to walk past me. I could tell that they'd been in the car with my mystery woman. Without thinking I reached out and tapped the girl on the shoulder. The guy walked a few paces on and then stopped to wait for her, so I thought I'd better make it quick. "Excuse me, but could you tell me the name of the blonde woman looking out the window of your car?"

After smiling wildly, she answered, "Yes. Her name is Rose." My informant continued to look back and forth between me and the girl, her heartbeat racing.

I reached for my wallet and took out one of my business cards and then scratched an impromptu poem on the back of it, adding my phone number at the bottom. "Could you please give her this for me and ask if she'd call me after dark in two days?"

"Um...sure, I guess," she replied.

The anxious feeling in my chest was the main reason I turned and quickly headed back into the club, but in reality, I could tell that this girl wanted to ask me a bunch of questions–questions that I couldn't and wouldn't answer.

Two days had passed, and this was the night that I hoped my dream girl would be calling. I had taken the evenings in between to talk to my sire, Evangeline, and let her know that I'd found someone that I was interested in and would hopefully be seeing very soon. I didn't need her permission, but since we weren't allowed to tell humans of our existence, I needed everyone to be aware that someone new would be coming around. Evie was happy to hear it. Her exact words were, "Oh Christian, I'm so happy that you've finally found someone that you want to share your life with." She then proceeded to tear up and gave me a series of smothering hugs as she beamed with pride.

I'd never really had a serious relationship since becoming a vampire. I fed out of necessity and never hurt anyone while doing it. Vampires have a sedative that flows from their fangs to make feeding pleasurable, but more importantly…forgettable. It's how we can exist in the human world; we have the means to make them forget. And yes, I'd dated before, but nothing serious or relationship worthy.

But ever since seeing Rose leaning out of that limo, the thought of a relationship was exactly what I had in mind. I couldn't explain why I was so drawn to this particular woman, but I knew from the moment that I caught her scent there was something special about her. The way it had taken every ounce of strength I had not to dart over to her car and crush my lips to hers that first night was something that had caught me off guard. She smelled like innocence and sweetness: like fresh cotton and sweet tarts, and sunshine and rain, all mixed together. I felt as if I was already in love with her. I knew that sounded dramatic, but after being alive for six hundred and two years, I knew when I'd found someone special.

I left the mirror and walked back towards my closet, discarding yet another shirt on the bed. For some reason even the simplest things like choosing my clothes and what cologne I would wear suddenly seemed like daunting tasks. I'd essentially dressed the same for centuries, always making it a point to adapt to the current styles. And since there was literally nothing I could do to change my appearance as I would look the same for all of eternity, picking the right clothes seemed oddly important. But...not as important as the need to attend to my drifting.

Drifting was something that happened to vampires when they experienced any kind of strong emotion. If they were hungry, angry, or aroused, their physical appearance actually drifted darker and then back to normal once the emotions had passed. It was something that made it easy to tell who was experiencing heightened emotions in the vampire community, but obviously it was something that we had to hide from the humans. How would anyone explain their hair and eyes changing colors? You simply couldn't.

If I fed and kept my emotions tightly reigned in, I should be able to avoid drifting in front of Rose. So after dressing in dark navy jeans, a light blue cotton button-up shirt, and a nice pair of hiking boots, I headed out to quench my thirst and prepare to meet the girl of my dreams. Hopefully, she would call.

CHAPTER FOUR

High School Sweethearts

(Rose)

After finishing breakfast, Mom and I headed to Kohl's to look for her swimsuits and an outfit for my date tonight. Well, hopefully I would have a date tonight. I wasn't sure what my plans were going to include since I hadn't actually made the call yet. But I was confident that Christian and I would be seeing each other soon, even if it wasn't actually tonight.

"What kind of outfit are you looking for?" Mom asked.

"I'm not really sure. A dress, I guess. Something casual, but not too boring. But nothing too over-the-top either." I didn't want to come off as a desperate slut, but

I wanted to show off my curves at the same time.

I watched as she slid dress after dress to the side of the rack, flinging the hangers like they had personally offended her. Finally, her perusing stopped and she held up a calf-length, strapless sundress. "How about this one?"

It was light turquoise blue with a simple print on it. The material was a rayon blend and should flow just right, hanging perfectly along my curves. This was the one. I had the perfect pair of tan wedges that would go great with it, and I could wear the choker that I'd bought recently as well. "Absolutely. It's perfect." *Wow, that was easy!*

Once we'd paid for our things, Mom and I headed to the pool. She was a swim instructor and worked at the local training facility. I knew that Mom wanted to give her new suits a test run, and since it wasn't time for the sun to go down yet, I actually welcomed the distraction. Anything to keep my mind off making the call that would hopefully be the beginning of something wonderful.

When we entered the large square foyer, Mom waved to the attendant who stood behind the counter. This area of the complex was surrounded by glass and full of light. "Hi, Andrew. We're gonna take a few laps in the indoor pool today, if that's alright. We'll be out before the next open swim session starts."

"Sure thing, Ms. Reynolds. Open swim doesn't start until six p.m., so you're good to go," he replied.

We both smiled and then made our way downstairs to the locker room. As I sat on one of the wooden benches that lined the room, I began to wonder what it would be like to meet the man I would end up marrying. Yes, I had high hopes for tonight. "So, Mom...how exactly did you and Dad meet? I'm assuming it wasn't by him handing you a card outside a nightclub." I shrugged my shoulders, feeling a little shy about the topic as I continued to undress.

"Well, no. No poems by the roadside, but he was pretty darn romantic. I was on the swim team for my high school, and he was at one of the meets. I remember after my first race, which I won," she said with a proud smile, "a friend said that she'd seen this guy checking me out and cheering me on, even though we were competing against his school." As Mom put her things in the locker, she continued the story. "I remember looking for him in the direction my friend had pointed, but didn't see anyone matching her description. Well...about an hour later when the meet had ended, I was heading to the bus when I saw a guy standing next to the sidewalk with a bouquet of fake flowers, and he was waving me over."

"Wait–Dad brought you *fake* flowers?" I laughed as I pulled on one of her new suits. It was nice being able to share clothes with your mother.

"Yes. Don't judge. It was the best he could do on short notice. Anyway....the closer I got, I realized he was really cute. When he told me that he'd run to the art room to try and make something creative but all he'd found were those fake flowers instead, my heart melted." She giggled as she finished getting dressed. "How sweet was it that he even tried to get me anything? At that time, most guys would have just flipped their collars and pulled a James Dean, trying to look all cool, assuming that I'd worship the ground they walk on. But your dad was different. He made an effort that got my attention, and that's what really impressed me."

"Oh my god. That is so cheesy, but definitely

thoughtful."

"I know! I told you he was a romantic. We started dating that month, and have been together ever since. We were each other's high school sweethearts."

I thought about Mom's story as I shuffled my feet along the damp, cold hall that led from the locker room out to the pool. I couldn't imagine being with someone for that long and still being in love, but suddenly it sounded like a pretty amazing goal to have. I didn't know what would happen with Christian, but in this moment, I actually felt like my heart was opening and I realized that I was truly ready to find love for the first time in my life.

I'd had plenty of boyfriends in the past, but I could admit that I hadn't been particularly serious or very open in my relationships. I didn't have a sad story as to why, other than the fact that I'd always been highly motivated to succeed. Starting junior year of high school, I had signed up for AP classes, so when I went into college, I actually entered as a junior, having attained two years worth of college credits already. This meant that I would be graduating early. I had always been passionate about setting goals and meeting them, and was pretty proud that I had accomplished that. But it wasn't without long hours and hard work, and as you can imagine, that put the boys on the backburner.

Mom's question brought me back to the present. "So, tell me more about Christian. What does he look like?"

"Oh man. He's gorgeous. Tall, blonde-highlighted hair, toned but not overly muscular. Um...I'd say just about perfect." I stared out the skylight as I floated on my back in the pool. "His eyes are like caramel swirled with honey. And he has a really sweet, gentlemanly demeanor."

"You got all that just from seeing him out the window?" She tried not to sound skeptical, but I could tell that she was probably worried that I'd get my hopes up and then be left disappointed.

"Yes, I did. I can't explain it, but when I watched him help that girl it just made my heart melt. And Jill said that he was really sweet when he spoke to her."

"Well, just keep it casual and don't talk about stuff that's too serious on the first date. And no messing around."

"Really, Mom? You think I'd just jump in bed with some guy on the first date?" *Actually, imagining how gorgeous Christian was, that didn't sound like a bad plan at all.*

CHAPTER FIVE

Good Time

(Christian)

After heading up the spiral staircase that led from our secure lair below ground, up and out from under the moveable dance floor, and into the actual club, I was met with jeers and smiles. My vampire brothers and sisters had already started giving me crap about seeing this new girl.

"So...where you gonna take *Rose* on your first date?" Bobby asked.

Bobby was the DJ here at the club, and he also happened to be my best friend.

"I'm not sure," I replied, "since she hasn't even called yet." I was getting nervous that she wasn't going to call at all. I'd thought about running into town to track her down, but I'd really rather not come off as the stalker-type right from the get-go.

"Well, if she *does* call, where are you gonna take her?" He just wouldn't let it go.

"I'll probably take her to dinner and then just walk around town. Is that acceptable enough for you?" No way was I going to tell him that I already had arranged everything, including reservations and a surprise after dinner.

"No. That is not acceptable. You need to show her a good time, and by that I mean, a *GOOD TIME!*" Everyone started laughing as we watched Bobby gyrate his hips around and around.

"Well, you can forget that. You know that I would never do that on a first date." I realized I sounded like an old stick-in-the-mud, but I didn't care. I would never expect a woman to "put out," as they say, on the first date or even on the twenty-first date. I was old-fashioned and refused to let myself fall into the modern way of "hooking-up" like Bobby had.

Just as I was about to say these exact words to him, my cell phone rang. Everyone went quiet. The anticipation in the air was palpable. I felt like such a girl; butterflies flapping in my stomach and palms sweating, I opened the phone. "Hello?"

CHAPTER SIX

Excited

(Rose)

Once Mom and I finished our workout, we got dressed and headed back to the house. Dad had spent the day doing yard work, and was now ready for a late lunch. I left them to it and headed for my room, wanting some time alone before I started to get ready.

I smiled as I hung my new dress from the hook on the back of my door, smoothing the material under my hands. After gathering all the accessories that I wanted to wear it with, I lay down on my bed and stared at the blank ceiling. I had to relax a little before I could process all of this. Here I was getting ready to call a complete stranger that I saw, not met, outside of a nightclub alongside the road. Suddenly my stomach was doing flip-flops. What if I was making a huge mistake?

I must have fallen asleep while contemplating everything because I suddenly found myself being woken up by my mom. "Rose. Wake up, sleepy head. It's almost dark. Did I wear you out in the pool today?" She sat down on the edge of the bed and gave my shoulder a little shake to make sure I was waking up.

"Yeah...I guess. I was just laying here staring at the ceiling and thinking about tonight, and I guess I dozed off." I pushed up on my elbows, and once my eyes finally adjusted to the changing light in my room, I found my mom staring at the ceiling. "What are you thinking about?" I asked her.

"Well, I'm thinking that we should paint your ceiling black."

"What? Why on earth would you want to do that?"

I was giggling by the time I fully sat upright.

"You'll see. But tomorrow, after you've debriefed me about how this date with Christian goes, we're starting a project." She winked as she casually strolled out of my room.

Oh yes, my date with Christian. I was so excited. I slung the covers back, jumped out of bed, and bounced towards the bathroom. I was going to have to hurry to get ready in time, since I had fallen asleep. I wanted to be dressed when I called Christian, in case he did actually want to meet up tonight.

Since I had already figured out everything I was going to wear, it really didn't take me too long to get dressed. I'd done my make up the same as usual, adding a little extra glittery eye-shadow on the upper arch of my eyelids, hoping to highlight their light blue color. I'd also decided to give my hair a slight curl on the ends, which was different from the straight style that I normally wore. Checking the full-length mirror on the back of my bathroom door one last time, I nodded. I was satisfied with my appearance. Now I just hoped Christian would be equally satisfied. *Stop stalling*, I thought to myself. It was time to make the call.

I walked across the room, the soft carpet cushioning my still bare feet, and grabbed his business card from the top of my dresser. After making my way to the bed, I sat down and took a few deep breaths, then dialed. He answered after only two rings. "Hello?"

"Hi, Christian. This is Rose. Rose Reynolds. You had asked my friend to have me call you tonight." Suddenly, I felt like a complete dumbass. What if he didn't remember seeing me or giving Jillian his business card? *Oh my god.* I was mortified.

I was seriously on the verge of hanging up when he

responded, "Hi, Rose. I'm so glad that you called. I wasn't sure if you would or not, seeing the unusual circumstances of our first encounter."

Oh thank goodness. He remembered, and he was happy that I was calling. *Woohoo!* "Yes, I'm sorry that I was unable to get out and actually meet you that night, but I was thrilled to get your note. It was very sweet."

"I'm glad you liked it. It was the best I could do on short notice." He laughed and then I heard a door close in the background. I could now hear the wind, so I assumed he had just left his house. "Speaking of short notice, I wondered if I would be able to actually see you tonight? No pressure though, I'll understand if you're unable."

"Actually, I had hoped for the same thing. Did you want me to come down there or did you have other plans?" *Yes!* This was going exactly like I wanted.

"I'd be more than happy to come pick you up, or you could just meet me at the restaurant. I thought we could have dinner at the steak house on the corner of Elm and 3rd. I've heard it's very good."

"Yes, that sounds perfect. I'll meet you there in say...twenty minutes?"

"Sounds great. I'll wait for you outside. And Rose...I really am thrilled you called."

"Me too. I'll see you soon."

CHAPTER SEVEN

First Impression

(Christian)

As soon as I hung up the phone, I tried to escape without seeing my vampire family again, but I wasn't so lucky. Bobby and Dominique had followed me outside when I had left the club to talk to Rose.

"So, the steak house on Elm and 3rd, huh?" Dominique asked. I knew she was just teasing me, but I really didn't have time to deal with their shit.

Answering dryly, I said, "Yes. The steak house on Elm and 3rd. I figured I could get a rare steak and force my way through dinner. I want a chance to really talk to this girl and thought dinner would be the best way to start. Do you have a different opinion?"

Shaking his head and holding up his hands in a we-give-up sort of gesture, Bobby answered for her. "No, no...that sounds like a great plan. Just don't be surprised if you see all of us peeking in the window from across the street." He and Dominique both busted up as they headed back towards the club.

Sighing heavily as I climbed in my '67 Mercury Comet Caliente, I could only hope that he was kidding. I heard the engine rumble to life and realized that I didn't drive this car as much as I would like to. There was just no need. My vampire speed could get me to most of the places I went to in a matter of seconds, but it sure felt nice–and normal, to actually be driving somewhere. And what was waiting for me at my destination made the trip even that much more enjoyable.

I made my way up the interstate towards Seela, the little town where Rose lived. I couldn't wait to actually meet her. As a matter of fact, I was so caught up in thinking about how to make a good first impression that I almost missed my turn off. Screeching the tires, I made the adjustment just in time and headed towards the section of town that now seemed like the most important place on earth.

As soon as I parked the car across from the restaurant, it took everything I had not to use my vampire speed to race across the street. Instead, I forced myself to calmly walk to our predetermined meeting place. The butterflies were an indication of how anxious and nervous I really was. It was glaringly obvious that it had been ages since I'd actually been out on a real date. Well, nothing like jumping in feet first, because here she came.

She was just as gorgeous as I remembered. Her hair held a little more curve to it than last time, and my god, those legs were just as sexy as I'd imagined. I watched her lock her car and walk in my direction, and I suddenly realized that keeping my drifting in check tonight was going to be an exercise in sheer willpower.

She was smiling as she hopped up onto the curb right in front of me. "Hi!"

My first instinct was to grab her and race away to somewhere private and sink my fangs into her neck. She was so sexy and smelled so good.

"Hello. It's nice to actually meet you, Rose." I held out my hand, hoping she'd take it. She did.

"It's nice to meet you, too."

Her smile was mesmerizing. So much so that I could barely think straight. "Um...are you ready to go in for dinner?" What a stupid question to ask outside of a restaurant. I mean, why else would we be here? I hoped I wasn't going to blow this.

"Absolutely. Let's go."

The confidence that she displayed as she led me into the restaurant immediately put me at ease. She was so sure of herself, and for a vampire who was six-hundred and two years old, I had been around some extremely confident people, but no one I had ever met could outshine this woman.

CHAPTER EIGHT

Table for Two

(Rose)

I was so excited that Christian had actually wanted to meet for dinner that I had raced downstairs after hanging up the phone, grabbed my purse, and headed straight for the car. Just as I was about to open the side door to the garage, Mom's voice rang out from the back door. "I take it your plans are a go with Christian?"

"Yep. We're having dinner here in town. I'll be home later. Love you, Mom."

"I love you too. I hope you have fun. Be careful and call if you need anything."

As I backed the car out of the driveway, I gave one last wave to Mom and Dad, who had now joined her at the back door. They stood there watching me with smiles on their faces as he wrapped her in his arms. It made me so happy to see how in love they still were after all these years. I hoped that I would someday find that kind of love. Suddenly, I was feeling the pressure of tonight's date.

I saw him the moment I rounded the corner. He had just stepped up onto the curb in front of the restaurant. I hoped that I wouldn't screw up my parallel parking. I took a few deep breaths and pulled my car to a halt. I didn't want to seem like a nervous Nelly, sitting there trying to get myself together for too long, so I forced myself out of the car right away and locked the door. I saw him watching me as I walked across the street, so I put as much sexy swagger into my stride as I could without looking like a runway model who was trying to work it too hard.

"Hi!" I said as I bounced up beside him.

"Hello. It's nice to meet you, Rose."

Oh damn, he has a sexy voice. An uncontrollable smile spread across my face as I took the hand he offered. "It's nice to actually meet you, too."

"Um...are you ready to go in for dinner?" he asked.

"Absolutely. Let's go." He hesitated for just a moment, and I found myself grinning from ear to ear. I took the lead and quickly pulled him into the restaurant before I embarrassed myself. The hostess took in an eye full of Christian before meeting my gaze. Who could blame her? He truly was drop-dead gorgeous.

"Table for two, under Christian," he said. That's when I noticed that he wasn't even giving the hostess a single glance. His eyes were sparkling and glued to mine.

My smile widened and I couldn't help but press my tongue to my teeth as I let out a slight giggle. I actually hated girls that did nothing but giggle in the presence of a guy, but oh my god–*this* guy had me wanting to laugh like a lunatic as we ran through fields of daisies. I was that ridiculously happy.

Once the hostess led us to our booth, which was perfectly situated in the quiet part of the restaurant, I thanked her and slid into my seat. Christian smiled and thanked her as well, and received a beaming smile in return along with a "let me know if you need absolutely anything" parting comment to which he didn't even respond.

"Would you like some wine?" he asked.

"I would love some, except for the fact that it might get you thrown in jail."

"Why would it get me thrown in jail? Are you a violent drunk who'd trash the place?" he teased.

"No, but I'm only twenty years old. Thanks for the

offer though." I smiled back at him as he set the wine menu off to the side.

"Oh, well that explains it. Sorry. I shouldn't have assumed. It just feels like I already know you, so I didn't think to ask your age."

"It's okay. Now that you know how old I am, it's your turn to share. How are old are you?"

"Yes, of course. Formal introductions. My name is Christian Royce, and I'm twenty-four years old. As you already know, I work at The Rising Pit. I'm their head of security."

"Cool. Well, I'm Rose Reynolds, and I'm a senior at Seela State University."

"Nice. What's your major?"

"History."

"What a coincidence. History was my favorite subject."

His dazzling smile and the sparkles in his eyes were pretty damn distracting, so I didn't even care if what he was saying was true or if he was just trying to score points. Either way, I was hooked.

"And I have to tell you, Rose, I'm a little nervous as I haven't been on a date in over five years." *More like fifty.* "And you are the first girl that I've ever taken to dinner."

"Really? Where did you take your other dates? The racetrack?" I tried to make light of the situation, but internally, I was doing my happy dance. He hadn't dated anyone in five years. *Crap, I wonder if there's something wrong with him?* "If you don't mind me asking, why haven't you dated anyone for five years?" *Please have a good answer.*

"No, I don't mind you asking at all. I guess you could say that I'm old fashioned and I am not in the habit of 'hooking-up', and everyone that I've encountered wasn't what I'd consider 'relationship material'. So, I've only had brief, non-serious acquaintances while I kept my eye out for the perfect girl." He winked at me as he picked up the menu.

Definitely a good answer.

I couldn't help but bite my lower lip in an effort to keep the biggest, goofiest grin from taking over my face. "So, I guess you're saying that you asked me out because you think I'm 'relationship material'?" I hoped that I wasn't digging a hole for myself. Mom had warned me not to talk about too serious of stuff on our first date, but Christian wasn't the only one who felt like we'd known each other forever. I was so comfortable talking to him, and even the vibe he gave off was one of genuine kindness. So, needless to say, I was really liking how things were going so far.

"Yes. That's exactly what I'm saying. When I saw you looking out that window, you were so beautiful, that

I just couldn't stop myself from asking you out. I would have come over myself, but since I was on duty, I had to get back inside. I just hoped that you would call, and I can't tell you how happy it made me when you did."

The waitress arrived just then asking if we were ready to order. Christian ordered a rare steak–*eeeww,* and I ordered the garlic shrimp fettuccine. After passing her the menus, we just sat quietly for a few moments staring at each other. I don't think I'd ever felt so connected and excited about someone before. I had told Mom that I wouldn't be jumping into the sack with anyone on the first date, but damn...if he asked, I don't think I would say no.

CHAPTER NINE

Making Plans

(Christian)

After Rose and I had gotten past the initial informatory part of our conversation, which included me giving her the fake last name that I used, and my estimated age, we ordered and then just sat there staring at one another. She was the most beautiful thing that I'd ever laid eyes on, and the moment I caught the scent of her excitement, I had to dig my nails into my thighs under the table in an effort to keep from drifting.

I would love nothing more than to bed this gorgeous woman tonight, but since that was never going to happen, I thought it best to change the subject...quick.

"So, tell me more about yourself. What does your

family do?"

I listened as Rose talked lovingly about her mother and father, sharing stories from her youth which painted a picture of the perfect family life. The conversation was great and we both enjoyed our meals, even though it was a bit of a struggle getting that steak down. It had been so long since I'd had to fake my way through an actual meal, but all in all things were going great.

As we finished our meal, I asked, "I wondered if you would like to take a walk with me after dinner? I have something that I'd like to show you just around the corner."

"Sure. That sounds great."

As I laid the money for the bill and tip on the table, I made sure that I was in complete control before reaching for Rose's hand for a second time. Again, she didn't hesitate to take mine in return. We walked out of the restaurant like a couple who'd been together for a very long time. It felt wonderful and perfect.

"I thought we could walk around the block and head to the festival in the park that's going on tonight."

"Oh, that's right. The movie festival. I love those. I wonder what's playing?"

I had already known what was playing, and as cliché as it was...I was interested to see what her reaction would be to Dracula. "I believe it's Dracula."

"Awesome! That's one of my favorites."

Damn, this girl just keeps getting better and better.

As we strolled around the block, we casually chatted about the town and how she had lived there her whole life. When we reached the park, we wove our way through the crowd and settled ourselves on a bench that was towards the back of the viewing area under one of the massive red maple trees. "Will this be okay? Can you see the screen from here?" I asked.

"Yes. It's perfect." And with that, she slid closer to me and I put my arm around her shoulders. It was that simple. Being with her felt so easy, and one-hundred percent right. *This truly was the perfect night.* We sat in silence as we watched the rest of Dracula under the full moon.

"I can't tell you how great this night has been for me." I tried not to sound like a complete lame-ass, but it was the truth. I hadn't experienced this kind of emotion in a long time, and I was pretty impressed with myself for keeping my drifting at bay throughout the evening. But...that all changed when she faced me and slipped her hand up around my neck as she leaned in to place her lips gently on mine.

I closed my eyes after making sure that hers were closed as well, and let the sensation of her soft lips

58

penetrate my brain. I knew that anyone walking by right now would see the previously blonde guy suddenly sitting here now with dark brown hair, but honestly...I couldn't care less.

Since Rose had initiated the kiss, I let her control the intensity. It was sweet and gentle, but had the makings of something that could turn fierce in a heartbeat. I never wanted it to end. But as she pulled back, I had to use all my willpower to blank out my emotions to make sure she found me drifted back to my normal coloring.

"That was for the perfect evening." She smiled and shyly ducked her head as she reached for her purse and started to stand.

I wanted so much to pull her back down onto my lap and kiss her senseless, but I was extremely happy with how things were going tonight and I didn't want to risk ruining anything. "You're right...tonight has been perfect. So, I was wondering if you'd be open to making plans for later this week?" *Please say yes.*

"I'd love nothing more."

CHAPTER TEN

He's the One

(Rose)

Once Christian and I had parted ways after reaching our cars and sharing a few more delicious kisses, I couldn't wait to get home to see if Mom was waiting up for me. I had to talk to her and see if the feelings I was experiencing were the same as what she had felt after meeting Dad. Because honestly, I don't think I had *ever* felt this way before.

I knew it had been kind of bold of me to lean in and kiss him first, but I just couldn't resist. The whole evening had been so amazing, and while sitting there in his arms at the park, I really did have the overwhelming feeling that we'd been together for years. So...I did it. I leaned in and gently placed my lips to his, and it was incredible.

As I pulled the car into the garage, I noticed a warm light radiating from the den window. *Yes, Mom's still awake.* After tiptoeing in my open-toed shoes through the dew-covered grass, I opened the back door and put my things down just as Mom stuck her head into the kitchen.

"So...how was it?" she asked, not even bothering with any small talk.

"Heaven. It was absolute heaven. Mom, he's sooooo nice, and gorgeous, and it felt like we'd known each other forever. I can't even explain it." I continued to gush about my feelings as we headed back towards the den. I flopped myself down onto the sofa, and met my mom's smile with one of my own. "I can honestly say that I've never been this happy in my life."

"Well, that's saying a lot, because as your mother, I can remember plenty of times that you've been extremely happy." She continued to smile as she made her way to join me on the couch. "I'm so thrilled you feel there's a connection there, but just be careful not to get your hopes up too high. Everyone always puts their best foot forward on a first date, but I say, until you hit the three-month mark you don't really know someone's true personality."

"Well, we've already made plans to see each other again later this week. And if things continue to go like I think they will...not only will we reach the three-month mark, but I could see three years, easy!"

Her eyes widened briefly and then a gentle and loving look settled on her face. "Rose, that's great. I'm truly happy for you, but again, please don't rush into anything, okay?"

"I promise I'll be careful. But for the first time in a long time, Christian has given me something else to be excited about besides school. It feels good. But don't worry, it's not like we're gonna rush off and get married or anything." I pushed off from the couch and began to make my way out of the den. "I love you, Mom. I'm gonna head to bed and hopefully have some juicy dreams about Christian."

She cupped her hands over her ears and shook her head. "TMI, TMI." Smiling as she followed me out of the den, she continued, "Alright. Sleep well, but tomorrow be ready to work. We're starting that project in your room, remember?"

"Are you seriously going to paint my ceiling black?"

"Yes. Yes I am. It's for a specific purpose though, so just keep your eye rolls to a minimum and wait and see what I have planned. You're going to love it, I'm sure."

Laughing, I waved my hand over my head as I headed down the hall. I wasn't kidding about wanting to have some good dreams about Christian, but what I truly wanted to do was get upstairs, change into my pajamas, crawl into bed, and give Christian a call. Our date may have been over, but he'd made sure to tell me that because of his work schedule he literally stayed up all night. So, we had made plans for me to call him as soon as I got settled at home. And since there was no way that I'd be getting him out of my head anytime soon, I figured I could spend the rest of my night talking to the man who would be inspiring my dreams instead.

CHAPTER ELEVEN

Mom's Project

(Rose)

After spending a couple of hours talking to Christian, I finally reached the point of exhaustion. He must have heard it in my voice because he said, "I can tell you're getting tired. Why don't you lay that beautiful head down and get some rest? I'll call you after dark tomorrow, because during the day, I'm dead to the world. Goodnight, Rose. Sweet dreams."

And oh boy, did I have some sweet dreams. Christian and I in Paris looking at the lights of the Eifel tower. Christian and I kissing outside of a Scottish castle. Christian and I riding in a gondola in Venice. I didn't want to leave this glorious dreamscape, but with

Mom rummaging around outside my bedroom door, my fanciful dreams were quickly put to an end. As I gradually woke up, all I could think about was that I would be seeing Christian in just one more day. Thank god for small miracles.

"Good morning," Mom announced as she cracked open my bedroom door. I sat up, propping myself up on the pillow. I watched her as she dragged some supplies in with her. Black paint, rollers, drop-cloths, and a large bag from the metaphysical store in town. Now I was getting nervous. Mom's project was about to hit full-swing.

"So we're really doing this?"

"Yes ma'am. But painting the ceiling's not all!"

"Oh goody...there's more." I rolled my eyes and gave her a goofy smile. "Would you like to elaborate?"

"Of course." After setting down her supplies, she spun around in a circle, her arms held wide. "We're going to create a nighttime wonderland."

I watched her turn around with her beautiful smile and sparkling eyes, and I just couldn't say no. I loved when Mom got one of her crafty ideas, but I wasn't exactly following what she had in mind. "Want to elaborate...more?"

She took a seat on my bed and continued. "We're going to paint your ceiling black, and then hang these beautiful crystals from it." She dug out a handful of crystal stars and moons in all sizes and colors and laid them across my bed. Then with a spark of wonder in her voice, she continued, "It will be beautiful, and you'll feel like you're sleeping under the twinkling stars every night."

I lifted one of the crystals in my hand and let in dangle in the sunlight. The rainbow it cast onto my wall was stunning, but I wasn't convinced it would have the same effect at night. But knowing my mother as I did, there would be no stopping her. "Cool idea. Let me get dressed and we can get started."

"I'll head down and make us some breakfast first, okay?" She breezed out of my bedroom, not waiting for a reply.

As I headed towards my bathroom, I noticed the little red light on my cell was blinking. I had a message. I felt the butterflies starting to stir again as I grabbed the phone. *I hope it's a message from Christian.* And it was. He had sent me a text just before dawn that read, "Thinking of you. Talk to you soon. Have a good day at school tomorrow, and call me as soon as the sun goes down. Love, Christian."

Love, Christian. I can't tell you how long I stared at that phrase. Feeling suddenly energized, I threw on my artsy coveralls and put my hair up in a quick ponytail, and then jogged down the stairs. "Smells good, Mom."

"I made cinnamon toast, bacon, and eggs." She smiled as she sat the plate in front of me and then grabbed one of her own, piled high with the same yummy goodness. "So, I heard you on the phone last night. Just couldn't get enough of Christian from your date, I take it?"

I wiggled my eyebrows at her as I took a bite out of my toast.

She laughed and shook her head. "Oh...young love. I remember it well."

We continued talking about boys and the gushy feelings they gave us while we finished breakfast, and then headed back to my room to start painting.

It had taken us most of the day just to paint the ceiling. Not because it was a particularly large room, but because we sucked at painting. I kept hitting the walls and having to do touch-ups, and even though Mom was in awesome shape, we had to take a lot of breaks because our arms kept getting tired from painting above our heads. Eventually we finished and decided we would head out for a late lunch while the paint dried. So, after we both showered and attempted to wash off all the black specks that decorated our hair and skin, we headed to the local pizza place.

As we were seated in our booth, I heard a familiar voice. "Hey guys, can we join you?" Jillian and her mom Adrienne were walking towards us.

"Absolutely," my mom answered.

Jillian and I had been best friends since we were little. She had moved here from Arizona when she was six, and we'd become best friends on her first day of school. We'd grown up together, enjoying the same things until the end of junior high. That's when I became extremely focused on my school work, and she became a volleyball queen. We'd remained best friends and had always supported each other in everything that we did, and right now, I couldn't wait to tell her about my date with Christian.

"I was so glad when you called, Loraine. Jillian and I were just watching movies to pass the day, and this was a great reason to take a break and get out of the house," Adrienne said.

"Of course. I figured if we were going to be enjoying pizza and talking boys, you two should join us."

I hadn't known Mom had called them, but it didn't surprise me. She knew me so well. So, for the next hour and a half, I gushed to my best friend and her mom about the amazing guy I had just met, and how I couldn't wait for our next date. They "oohhhed" and "aaahhhed" at all the romantic details, and loved the idea of watching a movie in the park while being wrapped in his arms. "He sounds just about perfect," Adrienne said.

"He is...I'm almost sure of it." I laughed and continued to answer her questions with a huge smile on my face, but suddenly I noticed that Jill was being quieter than usual. I didn't ask her about it because I didn't want to upset or embarrass her, but I figured that she was just a little jealous of all my "Christian talk." She was used to being the center of attention, so instead of talking about Christian, I directed the conversation to Mom and Adrienne and began to stuff myself with pizza.

"Well, I think our paint should be dry by now. It was nice to seeing you guys." Mom waved goodbye as I slide out of the booth.

Feeling a little disappointed at Jill's reaction, all I said was "Bye," and then followed Mom out the restaurant. We drove home in silence and then headed back up to my room to finish our project without conversation.

"Okay, are you ready to starting hanging your moons and stars?" Mom's tone was casual, but I could tell there was something on her mind.

"Did you notice how Jill got all quiet when I kept talking about Christian?"

Sighing, Mom stopped spreading the crystals on my bed, and just looked at me. "Yes, I did. I think she was a little jealous. Are you okay?"

"Yes and no. I just expected her to be happier for me. I don't want anything to come between me and Jill, but I'm not going to stop seeing Christian just because she's feeling insecure or upset that for once she's not the center of attention."

A loving smile spread across Mom's face, and she

stood up and hugged me. "When you choose a man over your best friend, it can be a scary thing. But, it is also the first sign that it may, in fact, be the start of a serious relationship."

I melted against her and felt the sting of tears that were threatening to spill, so I closed my eyes. "Thanks, Mom. I love Jillian, but for the first time in my life, I feel like everything else needs to come second, including her. I'm falling hard for Christian, and thanks for not making me feel silly about it."

"You're welcome, sweetie, and I'm so happy for you. Now let's make some magic." She pulled away from our hug and brushed her thumb gently over my cheek before moving towards my dresser to grab a sack full of small silver hooks. "You stand on your bed, and I'll hand you a hook. Just screw them in, and then I'll give you a crystal."

It took us over an hour to get all of them strung up, which ended up being perfect timing, as the sun had finally gone down. "Are you ready for this? It's going to be amazing," Mom said.

I wasn't convinced, but as soon as I lay down on my bed, Mom opened the curtains to let the moonlight flow in and I was speechless. She'd been right. I was amazed as I watched the beautiful little stars and moons twinkle and spin right here in my very own room. "Oh, Mom. It's beautiful." I lunged off the bed and into her arms. "I love it. I absolutely love it."

"I'm so glad. And, I love you, too. I'm so proud of the woman you're becoming, and I feel like this is just the start of some pretty magical things that will be happening in your life."

"I think you're right."

CHAPTER TWELVE

Freak You Out

(Christian)

I spent the next couple of days after my initial date with Rose trying to avoid the jokes and teasing from my family about how I'd fallen for a human. I had not been successful, so when Bobby approached with a smirk on his face, I braced myself for yet another jab.

"So, tonight's the first night you're gonna see Rose again, right?" Bobby asked.

"Yes. Why?"

"Oh, no reason. I just wondered what exactly you were planning to do for your second date." Bobby puckered his lips and put his hands behind his head as he wound his hips around and around.

"You've really got to get some new moves." I shoved past him and headed towards Evie's office.

"Oh, I can show you some new moves if you need some help," he yelled just as I slammed the door shut.

After settling myself in the chair in front of Evie's desk, I said, "I need to warn you that I might beat the shit out of Bobby later."

She laughed as she offered me a glass of dark red blood. "Well, just don't get blood on the carpet."

I shook my head and politely declined. I couldn't stand drinking blood from a glass. Even if it was heated up, it just didn't taste the same. Plus, I never knew which donor Evie was currently using for her supply, and I didn't like *not* knowing where my food had come from. "I've invited Rose down tonight to come see me during my break. I told her that I didn't have much time off work so we'd have to work around my schedule. I wanted to appear as if I have a normal job and responsibilities. Is that alright?"

"Yes, that's fine. But you know you can come and go as you please, so you don't have to pretend your boss is such a tyrant who won't give you a day off." She smiled as she set the glass back down on her desk.

"I know, but since Rose isn't twenty-one, and I'm really not ready for her to meet everyone just yet, I thought this would be a good compromise. I suppose I could continue to see her outside of here, but I don't want her to feel as though I'm hiding my work from her. This way we still get to see each other, and her curiosity is satisfied."

"That sounds reasonable, but you know that we are all going to want to meet her sooner rather than later. Maybe I'll host a company mixer for just employees and their guests next month. How does that sound?"

I could tell that she was chomping at the bit to meet Rose. Hell, they all were. "That sounds just fine. And thanks for not rushing me, Evie."

I stood as she gracefully made her way around the desk and enveloped me in a hug. "You were my first son, Christian, and I'm beyond happy for you. Take all the time you need."

Just as I left Evie's office, I received Rose's text. "I'm almost there."

I had told her to text me when she was close so I could meet her outside. I didn't want her running into anyone without my protection. I knew all the vampires who came to The Rising Pit were decent people and would never hurt Rose, but I wasn't willing to take that chance. Besides, the thought of someone else sinking their fangs into my girl threatened to send me into a fighting rage.

As normal vampires, we couldn't kill each other. Only our Sire had the poison of true death, and therefore the ability to eliminate us. But, because of our super-strength and speed, our fights tended to be epic. It was rare for vampires to fight amongst themselves though, and the only time that it happened was usually over territory, which sometimes included humans. As archaic as it seemed, I definitely felt that I had a claim to Rose. In my mind...she was mine.

I watched her pull into the parking lot. My veins were sizzling with anticipation. Our first date had been perfect, and the conversation we had that same night had only solidified my feelings for her. But since this was the first time we'd seen each other since, I was feeling a little apprehensive about how things would go. Especially since in the back of my mind all I could see was my vampire family rushing out of the club's door and bombarding us with questions and embarrassing the crap out of me.

"Hi, gorgeous," she said, just before throwing her arms around my neck and kissing me gently. *Guess things are going to go just fine.*

"Well, hello to you too, beautiful." I knew I was smiling like an idiot, but the fact that she seemed just as excited to see me as I was to see her only made me want to smile more. "How was your trip down? Did you have any trouble finding the place again?"

"Nope. Your directions were perfect, just like you."

As she started to close her eyes and lean in for another kiss, I lifted her off the ground and spun us around. The sound of her laughter was like sweet music to my ears. "Since you're not twenty-one we can't go inside the club, so do you mind if we just hang out in my car?" I knew it sounded like a lame pickup line, but I just wanted to get her inside my car before another vampire in the area smelled her and came to check things out.

"Sure, that sounds great."

I felt more relaxed once we were sitting inside my car, so I reached out to hold her hand. It felt phenomenal being able to touch her again, and to be able to talk face to face. We spent the next fifteen minutes talking about random things, like how long I had worked here, and whether I liked it or not. She asked if the weird hours bothered me, and if I ever thought about doing something else. I hated lying to her about such stupid little details, but I really had no choice. Only when she seemed to drift off into her own thoughts did I worry that my lies weren't convincing enough. Then, suddenly she leaned forward and kissed me, and this time with a little more heat.

"I'm sorry. I love talking to you, but watching your

mouth move is a little distracting." She smiled shyly, but I could tell from the heat in her eyes and the sudden rise in excitement that she really didn't want to listen to any more of my stories.

I studied the planes of her beautiful face: the luscious contour of her lips, the mesmerizing sparkle of her light blue eyes, and the smooth perfection of her long blonde hair; I too was suddenly done with small talk. I leaned in, threaded my fingers into her hair, and pulled her lips to mine. The kiss only lasted a few seconds before she broke away and climbed into the backseat. I wanted to laugh, but not because she was being funny or silly, but because I was so happy my undead heart felt like it was going to explode. She was so confident and secure in her sexuality, and obviously she knew what she wanted, and that was damn sexy. I knew we wouldn't be going all the way in the backseat of my car, but just the thought of being able to explore Rose and the level of our connection had me worried that keeping my drifting at bay was going to be a *huge* problem tonight.

"Sorry. Does this make you uncomfortable?" she asked.

This time I did laugh out loud as I climbed into the backseat to join her. "You're asking a guy if making out with a beautiful girl in the backseat of his car makes him uncomfortable? Um...no. It makes me the luckiest man in the world."

Her smile not only lit up the backseat of my car, but also my heart. With a serious look on her face, she continued, "I don't expect us to jump straight into the sack, but the connection I feel with you is unexplainable. I know this will sound weird, but it's almost as if there's something magical about it. I don't know...like I said, I can't explain it. I know this is only our second date, but for me it feels like we've known each other forever. I just hope that doesn't freak you out."

I took her hands in mine and looked deep into her eyes. "Rose, you don't have to worry about doing anything that is going to freak me out. I'm sure that most people wouldn't understand it, but I feel exactly the same way. You're right, there is something magical when it comes to the way I feel about you. It's like we were together in another life or something. Everything with you is so easy and natural, and I love how confident you are. A lot of people have a tendency to deny what's happening to them, but I'm glad we can both accept our feelings and not be afraid of them."

I caught her as she threw herself into my arms, hugging me as though her life depended on it. "Christian, you make me feel so comfortable and safe. I can honestly say that this is the first time that I've ever felt *ready* to start a relationship." She pulled away from the hug and with a teasing glint in her eyes, she said, "And I have to admit, I've never been as turned on by a man as I am by you."

That was the last thing we said to one another for quite some time. Because from that point on our bodies and mouths were otherwise occupied. The feel of Rose in my arms and the intensity of our kisses was something that I'd never experienced before. I was thankful that there weren't any lights in this part of the parking lot, because if there had been, then I'm sure she would have seen my drifted appearance. Instead, our eyes were closed or it was just so dark that she really couldn't tell the difference. I truly was the luckiest guy in the world.

* * * * *

From that day on, Rose and my relationship only grew. She would come visit me during my breaks at least a couple times a week, and every couple of weeks I would take her out on a real date, using the excuse of needing to wait for my paycheck to do something special. I just loved how normal everything was progressing. We had decided that we weren't going to sleep with each other until the time was right, because as intense as our feelings were, just talking and exploring each other was the perfect way to justify those feelings without throwing sex into the equation. Plus, if we were to actually have sex, I didn't think I would be able to control my urge to bite her, and since that would expose my secret–having sex was just not an option.

CHAPTER THIRTEEN

Dying to Ask

(Rose)

Christian and I had been seeing each other for about a month and a half now. I would almost venture to say that we were in love, even though neither of us had said it yet. We weren't having sex, but I was happy with that decision. It just made our conversations and the times we spent together that much more real. Our relationship wasn't about sex, though if our makeout sessions were any indication, our sex life was going to be amazing when it finally did begin.

But tonight, I had other plans. While spending all of my extra time with Christian was certainly wonderful, it was definitely taking its toll. I was dreadfully behind in all of my classes, and I had a paper due this week. I refused to let all my hard work go down the drain just because of a guy. So, I had bit the bullet and told Christian that I couldn't come down tonight because I had made plans with Mom to stay late after school in order to get some research done in the library. She was working late, conducting a class at the swim complex, and agreed to pick me up when she was done.

I was walking out of the library when my phone rang. "Hi, honey. Look I'm sorry, but this session is running late and I need you to take the bus over to meet me here instead. Is that going to be okay?"

"Sure, Mom. No problem. Just give me the address again." I quickly rummaged through my bag to grab a piece of paper and a pen to jot down the address. "Okay, got it. Looks like I should be there just after dark."

"Perfect. Just head around to the outdoor pool

when you arrive. Thanks, honey. I'll see you soon."

The bus ride went by pretty fast, and I arrived just after dark as expected. Walking around this huge complex was a little freaky at night, so when I approached the pool, and didn't hear anything, but instead saw thrashing waves in the pool, my nerves were shot.

"Mom?" I called out. There was no answer. I slowly walked towards the pool but stopped only after two steps because once I looked closer, I saw my mom and a guy struggling underwater. *Oh god, please no!*

I had never been faced with any kind emergency situation, so even though I wasn't proud of it, I was panic stricken and completely frozen. I couldn't move or scream until the moment the waves in the water started to clear.

What I saw was enough to scare me into motion. I

ran back around the corner of the building and hid while I watched as a man climbed out of the pool carrying my mother in his arms with his mouth plastered to the side of her neck.

Holy shit, my mom is having an affair. My legs almost gave out, dropping me to the ground. I was suddenly cold as ice and terrified to move because as I looked closer, I could tell that he wasn't kissing the side of her neck, but instead had sharp teeth that appeared to be piercing her instead. What I had first thought were sensual kisses were actually long drags of sucking. Then a thought hit me that changed my world. *Dear lord, a vampire is drinking from my mom.*

I finally, quietly, sunk to the ground, not knowing what to do or think. It felt like I was going to pass out. At first, I was so scared and feared that this monster was hurting my mom that tears instantly filled my eyes, but suddenly my anger trumped the fear and I started to look around for anything made of wood that I could slam into this asshole's heart. I wanted to scream when the man finally removed what could only be called fangs from my mom's neck. But then, as he laid her on one of the chaise lounges next to the pool, I witnessed how he gently brushed the hair out of her eyes. The kindness in his actions left me dazed and confused. Mom sat up with a smile on her face and waved as the man started to walk away. I was so relieved to see that she was still alive that I accidentally sucked in a quick breath. The man's head spun in my direction and suddenly I was being stared down by a pair of intense, dark eyes.

After a moment, he crooked his finger at me, indicating for me to come to him. I was still frozen in fear and literally couldn't move. The next thing I knew he was standing right in front of me. Only a split-second had passed, and I hadn't even seen him move, but there he was, dripping wet, towering over me with a cocky smirk on his face.

"Hi. You must be the daughter." His voice was deep and sexy, just like the rest of him. I couldn't believe that I had had those thoughts about a man who had just been holding my mother so intimately, but I couldn't deny reality. The guy appeared to be in his mid-thirties, with dark brown hair and eyes to match. He was tan and muscular, and probably about 6' 4". He looked like sex-on-a-stick.

"Yes, I'm her daughter. Who the hell are you?" I had finally gotten myself under control and stood up to face him, though my courage had run for the hills. This was definitely going to be a workout for my acting skills.

"I think the question you want to ask is, 'What are you?', am I right?" He had a mocking glint in his eye, and that damn cocky grin was still plastered to his face.

"I'm not stupid. I know what you are. You're a vampire."

His grin widened. "Are you scared?"

"Should I be?" I tried to bolster myself so that the fear I was feeling wouldn't come across in my shaking voice.

He stared at me for a long time then gave a slight *hmph*. "No, beautiful, you have nothing to fear from me. One a night is all I can handle."

I hated that his *one* had been my mom, but I was damn glad that he would be leaving me alone. "Did you hurt her?" Now that I felt somewhat safe, I had a shit-ton of questions that I was dying to ask him. Well, maybe dying wasn't the right word to use.

"No, I didn't hurt her, and she won't remember anything about tonight," he explained. "What about you?

Should I bite you and make you forget?" He seemed genuine in his question.

I tried not to shiver, but the goose bumps his question produced spread up my arms. "No. I don't want to forget. Actually, I have a lot of questions that I would love to ask you." I don't know why, maybe it was the brain-numbing fear or the years I'd spent researching as a history major, but in that moment the strangest thought of, *What an amazing paper I could write with his help*, drifted through my brain. Seriously. Was I debating asking a vampire to help me get a good grade on my history paper? He'd probably kill me for being so lame.

He turned around and saw that my mom had gotten up from her chaise and was starting to gather her things. "Why don't you meet me back here tomorrow night and I'll answer some of your questions?"

"Really? Or is this some kind of trick to get me here

so I can be the one you feed on tomorrow?" I was excited but not stupid. I wondered if crosses or stakes would actually work on this guy. Not that I'm Buffy, but a girl could try.

"No trick. I do, however, enjoy the taste of your mother's blood. It's different than any other that I've ever experienced. So once you spend the evening with her and realize that I'm telling the truth and that I didn't hurt her in any way, as long as I can continue to feed on your mom...I'll be willing to answer your questions. Is that something that you can handle?" He extended his hand as if preparing to shake on a deal.

"Okay. But if Mom shows any signs of being hurt or acting weird then you'll never see us here again." It was a lame threat because he could probably just follow us home or find us whenever he wanted, but I had to make sure he understood that if he had hurt my mom in any way, the deal was off.

"Deal." He shook my hand and then started to walk away. "Oh. One more thing. What's your name?"

"My name is Rose. What's yours?"

"Terrance. My name is Terrance."

CHAPTER FOURTEEN

Desensitized

(Rose)

Once I got Mom home, I offered to cook. Dad had a work meeting tonight that included dinner, so it was just going to be the two of us. All throughout our meal I watched her so closely that I thought my eyes were going to pop out of my head. She seemed perfectly fine and acted as though everything was normal. *Normal, what a joke.* But for just having discovered that vampires were real, I thought I was handling things pretty damn well.

I suppose with all the vampire lore that I studied in history, and with a new vampire movie or book popping up every other week, I, like the rest of society, had become desensitized. I wasn't sure if that was a good thing or a bad thing, but since I hadn't run away screaming at the top of my lungs that vampires existed, which would probably only have landed me in a loony bin–I was thinking it was a good thing.

After dinner, I climbed into bed with Mom under the premise of watching a movie, but really it was so I could keep an eye on her. She seemed to be doing fine. She didn't even have any puncture wounds where Terrance had bitten her. That was definitely something I was going to have to ask him about.

I met Terrance back at the pool the following night just like we had planned. Mom didn't know I was there as I hid behind the edge of the massive brick building. I kept my eyes on the pool expecting Terrance to creep towards my mom from the shadows, but suddenly, after hearing a noise, I turned to find him walking up behind me along the building instead. For a second I thought he was going to go back on his word and feed from me, but he didn't.

We sat down with our backs against the wall and started talking. It was all so surreal. He explained how vampires weren't the bad, evil villains of lore, and how every night they only fed on one person, and only took their fill. He told me that their powers let them make the feeding process an enjoyable act for both vampire and human, and it also allowed them to compel the human so that they didn't remember anything that had happened. He had said that these "powers" came from a sedative that flowed from their fangs. *How cool.*

Everything was going great, but I couldn't help the feeling of dread and uncertainty that filled my chest when he finally asked if it was alright to go feed from my Mom. But, since she'd been fine the night before, it wasn't like he'd lied to me about anything yet, so I decided to trust him. Plus, I didn't want to back out of my end of the deal and make him so angry that he decided to kill us both instead.

He told me to stay behind the building, so I did. She waved at him as soon as she saw him walking towards her. She started back towards the pool when he shook his head and gestured for her to take a seat on the chaise instead. She did so immediately.

I watched as he made his way around the back of the chair and sat down gently beside her. It took everything I had in me not to run over and beg him to stop, but in the next instant Terrance had sunk his fangs into my mom's neck and began to drink. I covered my mouth to hold in my scream and immediately looked away.

When he was done, which only took a minute or so, he laid Mom back on the chaise like last time, but instead of her getting up to gather her things, she just lay there instead. I started to panic and ran towards them. "What did you do? You said you wouldn't hurt her."

"I didn't hurt her. I just used my sedative to make her sleep for a little while so we could finish our conversation. I thought you might have some more questions."

"Oh, okay." He was right. I did have a lot more questions. The first of them being, why did my mom think she knew him?

"The first time I fed on her, I used my sedative to make her think I was one of her swim students. Since I don't have to breathe underwater, I sometimes submerge us in case anyone walks by. I'm able to control the flow of blood with my sedative so there's no mess, and if anyone see us while we're underwater, I'll have time to stop feeding and make it look like we were just doing some underwater training. And before you freak out, I always make sure she's never under too long."

"Freak out" was an understatement.

Terrance spent the next half hour talking me out of a panic by explaining a few specifics that came with being a vampire. Like how the puncture wounds close because of their sedative. Apparently, it is "programmable" and can not only be used for memory stuff, but for pleasure and healing as well. He also explained how vampires didn't burn in the sun, but fell into a deep sleep at its rising instead, along with a lot of other interesting facts.

When Mom started to wake, Terrance said goodbye and asked if I'd like to meet again tomorrow. After pondering if I should come just to watch over Mom, since apparently, she was his donor of choice, I decided that I needed some time to process everything and told him that I'd meet him again in a couple of days. At this point, I felt confident that he wouldn't hurt her because he had said that her blood tasted better than anything he'd ever tasted before. While that kind of creeped me out at first, I quickly noticed how gentle he was with her, and since she seemed fine after his feeding, I felt confident taking this time for myself. Besides, I had a date with Christian tomorrow night.

CHAPTER FIFTEEN

Revelation

(Rose)

It suddenly became a habit to keep a close eye on Mom, and to make sure she didn't show any negative signs from Terrance's feedings. But she always seemed perfectly fine. She went about her days as usual, and I decided that I could do no less.

School was normal, but I just couldn't seem to focus. *Gee, I wonder why?*

I kept thinking about everything that Terrance had told me, and yet how normal of a person he seemed to be. It was so hard to wrap my head around the fact that he was a honest to god vampire. Cringing, I wondered if I'd be struck down for using those two words in the same sentence.

As soon as the final bell of the day rang, I headed towards the restroom to freshen up before I headed down to Christian's for our "date." At this point, the dates were more like makeout sessions, but trust me—I wasn't complaining. We'd sit in the backseat of his car and talk about anything and everything, but inevitably, we'd end up in each other's arms and believe me when I say, there was no other place I'd rather be.

A bunch of girls in sportswear and ponytails busted into the restroom, rousing me out of my love-dazed thoughts. I spotted Jillian amongst the crowd and suddenly felt nervous. Not only did I feel guilty for not spending time with my best friend lately, but also because we never really talked about what had been up with her at the pizza place. I think I just didn't want to know.

"Hey, Jill. You heading to practice?"

"Sure thing. What are you up to? I haven't seen you much lately...I miss you." She threw her arms around me, which made me feel tons better. At least she wasn't mad at me for being too busy, since obviously she was pretty occupied with her team at the moment.

"I miss you too. I've just been hanging out with Christian, and working out with Mom at the pool a lot." No way could I tell her that I was currently spending time with yet another new guy that involved me meeting him after dark.

"Okay, well, have fun with Christian. I've gotta go kick some ass on the court!" Her whole team whooped and hollered as they bounced their way out of the restroom, leaving me to stare at myself in the mirror, wondering just how dense I could possibly be.

I was suddenly having an epiphany. Thinking about

Terrance needing to meet me after the sun had set had me putting two-and-two together. How interesting that Christian and I could never meet unless it was after dark as well? And why was he always so vague when it came to talking about any other job before this job that required him to work nights? He was also the only person I'd ever met that ate *everything* rare and practically bleeding on the plate.

Holy shit! I was dating a vampire. He had to be, and I knew one sure fire way to find out. I grabbed my cell and dialed Christian's number.

"Hello?"

"Hi, Christian. I'm just calling to let you know that I'm going to be a little bit late. I got held up at school and I still need to grab a bite to eat before I head down." I didn't want to cancel all together, but first...it looked like I would be meeting Terrance tonight after all.

After dumping all my makeup back into my purse, I made a beeline to my car–Mom had let me take it to school today since I would be headed to Christian's tonight. But this was a detour I had to make first. I drove straight to the swim complex and found Terrance waiting in the shadow of the trees just beyond the pool while my mom finished her last lesson of the day. I stood behind the corner of the building and waved him over the moment he noticed me. He was at my side in two seconds with a worried look on his face.

"Rose, is everything alright? You look upset, and your heartbeat is racing."

"I have to ask you something, and I want the truth. Do you know a vampire named Christian Royce?"

I knew the answer the instant that he dropped his head. After sliding down to the ground, we took our usual seats with our backs to the building and he told me the one thing that I never expected to hear.

"Yes. I know Christian. Royce is the last name that he uses in the human world, but we really don't have last names once we're turned. We are part of the same clan and live at The Rising Pit. How did you meet him?"

After the air left my lungs, I answered, "I've been dating him for the last month and a half. Why have I never seen you there?"

"I choose not to feed in the vicinity, and prefer to come into town instead. Christian has always fed close to home," Terrance explained.

I knew from the jealous feelings that raced through me at the thought of Christian touching another person, I wouldn't be breaking things off with him. Vampire or not...I was sure that I was falling in love him. And, based on my conversations with Terrance, I was certain that Christian wouldn't hurt anyone, so I really couldn't be angry at him for feeding on humans in order to survive. He couldn't help what he was.

Even though I could barely process that my boyfriend was a vampire, I suddenly felt much better. I was excited to tell him that he didn't have to keep it a secret any longer. "Well, I guess it will be a big surprise for him tonight when I tell him I know what he is."

"No. You can't!" Terrance exclaimed as he shot to his feet.

Panicked, he said, "If you reveal that you know vampires exist, you could get us both killed." He went on to explain that I had to hide my thoughts around other vampires, making sure that I only focused on the events that were immediately happening around me.

This seemed like an impossible request, and one that I wasn't sure if I could pull off. But I decided that I needed to know how keeping this secret was going to affect Christian and my relationship before I made any rash decisions. So, following Terrance's advice, planning to guard my thoughts and keep this revelation to myself, I went to see Christian.

On my way down, I had a series of panic attacks and almost turned the car around multiple times. I was so completely nerve-wracked, and I thought for sure there was no way that I was going to be able to keep my thoughts from him. But apparently, I was pretty good at hiding things from people, because he didn't notice a thing.

Our date went off without a hitch. The fact that I knew he was a vampire only heightened the emotions I was feeling. He didn't act or feel any differently and I realized in that moment that not only would I not be breaking up with him, but that I wanted to spend eternity with him. *Talk about a life changing revelation.*

I didn't see Terrance for a couple of days because what I had to think about deserved some serious consideration. Once I had made my decision, I met with Terrance and finally asked the question that I was dying to know. "So how exactly does someone become a vampire?"

"Well, it's pretty standard stuff, really. A vampire bites and feeds on a human until they've been fully drained, then the human feeds from the vampire in return. The human dies and is then reborn as a vampire in a matter of hours."

Standard indeed. No big surprises there. So, after a few more weeks of contemplating and finally admitting that I was, in fact, in love with Christian and that those feelings weren't ever going to change, I had made up my mind that I wanted to become like him so we could be together forever. I asked Terrance if he would be willing to change me, and he agreed.

"Okay, but here's the deal. No one can know that we know each other or that I'm going to change you. This isn't the usual way that these types of things happen, and by not following the rules, that puts us both in a lot of danger."

"Then what is the normal way? If there was a way to do this without breaking any vampire rules, and as long as I could keep it a surprise from Christian, I would do it."

"There is no other way. I told you we're in serious danger for you even knowing vampires exist. It's not like you can just walk in and ask everyone to take a vote. Traditionally, when a vampire wants to add someone to our clan, the whole clan has to vote on it, since everyone gets to have a say as to whom they want added to the family. But don't worry, as long as you can keep it a secret, I'll change you because I know that everyone will be happy, and Christian will be thrilled with this surprise. I may be in trouble at first, but I'll deal with it."

With that settled, the plan was for me to graduate college, and once I was moved out of my childhood home, he would change me and I would surprise Christian with the fact that we could now be together forever.

I couldn't wait.

CHAPTER SIXTEEN

Life was Over

(Rose)

After the decision had been made that I would become a vampire and surprise Christian with my transformation, life went back to normal. Normal, but better. Everything now held a newfound excitement for me. My dates with Christian were fantastic because knowing that I would never be without him gave me such internal happiness that it felt like I was walking on clouds whenever we were together. He finally expressed his love for me as well, and continued to display it in the most traditional ways: flowers, love notes, jewelry, etc., and constantly told me that he never wanted to live without me. That was something that I loved hearing, because in just under a year, he was going to be getting his wish.

Tonight's date had been especially great because Christian had told me that his boss, Evangeline, was going to be hosting a company mixer and all the employees were supposed to bring dates.

Though he never let on, it was obvious that this was his way of introducing me to his clan and I couldn't have been more excited. If he wanted me to meet them, then that meant at some point he was probably planning to have them vote as to whether I could become one of them, just like Terrance had explained.

"Absolutely, I would love to meet everyone you work with." I accepted the invitation and then kissed him goodnight as it was really late. I headed home, realizing that it was just after two in the morning. I hoped that I wouldn't wake up Mom and Dad, but Mom had a tendency to wait up for me, even though I was a grown woman. I didn't mind though, and if she was up, I would get to tell her about Christian inviting me to his "company mixer" next weekend.

The moment that I turned the corner at the end of my street, my vision was filled with blaring red and blue lights. It only took a couple seconds for me to realize that the ambulance and cop cars were centered around my house.

Oh no!

I had no idea what was happening. *I hope my dad didn't have a heart-attack,* was the first thought that crossed my mind. He always worked so hard, and lately he'd had to attend a lot more late and out of town meetings.

I parked the car down the street and ran towards the house as fast as I could. I tried talking to the first policeman I saw. "What's happened?"

"Miss, you need to get back in your car and head on

home," the cop politely stated.

"This is my home!" I screamed as I pushed my way past him and started across the yard.

"Rose!" My dad's voice rang out, and in the same instant my heart dropped. If he was running towards me, then something had happened to Mom.

From the tear streaks that coated his face, I knew it was bad. I stopped in my tracks halfway across the lawn and froze. By the time he reached me, everything had gone silent. It was like my ears were suddenly filled with cotton, and the whole world had started to operate in slow-motion.

The moment Dad reached me, he wrapped me in his arms and we fell to the ground. "Rose. She's gone. Your Mom's gone," he sobbed.

It wasn't the cold dew on the grass that caused my goose bumps, but the utter terror of what he'd just said to me. There had to be a mistake. I had just talked to Mom early tonight when I told her that I was going to be later than usual. There was no way that she could be dead.

"Sir, if you and your daughter would come with us, we have a few questions for you," the same officer said.

We were led into the house, and then instructed to take a seat in the living room. I was so lost in my head that I didn't even hear the police as they started asking my dad questions about what had happened. But once I was able to regain a small amount of focus, it became clear that someone had broken in and killed my mom when she'd come out of her room and spotted them. Dad said that he hadn't heard anything, but that when he woke up and found the bed empty, he'd got up to check on Mom and found her in the hallway, just outside their bedroom.

Dad continued to explain that it looked like she had just passed out, as there wasn't any blood, but when he tried to wake her, he realized that she wasn't breathing and called 9-1-1.

Apparently when the ambulance arrived and began examining the body, they had found two small puncture wounds on her neck, and requested my dad's permission to do an autopsy to pinpoint the cause of death.

After hearing this, the first thought that crossed my mind was, *Terrance.*

That son of a bitch no good vampire followed my mom home and killed her after feeding one last time. *Oh god, what if he turned her?*

I immediately realized that my train of thought didn't make any sense, because if Terrance *had* turned my mom, her body wouldn't be here. He would have taken her with him so they could complete the process, and so that he could be there when she woke as a vampire. No, this wasn't right. Plus, Terrance had always treated my mom like something he cherished, so why would he kill her? Something just wasn't adding up. Terrance couldn't have been the one who killed my mom.

I continued to ponder all the possibilities of what could've happened because there was no way that two puncture wounds to the neck was a normal cause of death. As a matter of fact, I heard them rule it a "freak accident" as they finished up their interrogation and began to clear the scene.

My attention was suddenly snapped into focus as I saw my mom's body being wheeled out the front door in a body bag. My dad quickly grabbed me and forced me to look away.

My mom's life was over, and so was mine. How was

I supposed to live without her? As the tears started to flow and the authorities finally left us alone, I sank into my dad's embrace. As devastated as I was, listening to him cry over the loss of his wife was what pained my heart the most.

After that night, everything changed. My dad took a sabbatical from work and pulled me out of school while we tried to process everything. He made funeral arrangements and had meetings with lawyers and insurance people all while insisting that I stayed glued to his side.

It quickly became clear that Mom's death had turned Dad into a scared, over-protective father. The only time I was able to grieve on my own was when it was time for bed or when I used the restroom. He wouldn't let me see Christian anymore, and since I practically never left the house without him, I never saw

Terrance again either. It had only been a month, but there was no end in sight to what I liked to call my "official lock-down." God, I missed my mom so much.

The only thing that made me happy was thinking about Christian. We talked on the phone as much as we could, and as harsh as it sounded, the fact that we would never have to go through something like this made me happy. I was still devastated that my mom was dead...but I was going to live forever.

Other books available in The Rose Trilogy:

Scent of a White Rose – Book 1

Blood of a Red Rose – Book 2

Death of a Black Rose – Book 3

Praise for *Scent of a White Rose*

"...everything about Scent of a White Rose was such a fresh new concept when it came to vampires, actually it was just a whole new concept in general for the paranormal genre! This is a read any paranormal lover should read!" ~ YA-Aholic

"Tish adds her own unique spin that makes Rose and Christian's story intriguing. The plot twists will definitely have you turning the pages to see what is going to happen next." ~ The Book Lovers Realm

"*Scent of a White Rose* is not the plain Jane girl meets vampire and falls in love story...I will tell you that you should add this book to your TBR list." ~ The Book Nympho

"Thawer managed what I thought was an impossible feat. She was able to put yet another new spin on the age old vampire tale." ~ The Bookshelf Sophisticate

www.ingramcontent.com/pod-product-compliance
Lightning Source LLC
Chambersburg PA
CBHW060625130626
46555CB00002B/671